Love's First Stage

Trish Perry

ISBN: 9798670221702

i

Chapter One

Two seconds after the old man cursed and hung up on Anna, she closed her eyes, exhaled, and spoke to no one in particular.

"One more angry customer today, and I do believe my head will explode."

Her cubicle mate, Cheryl, had just returned from the office kitchen. She set down Styrofoam cups of steamy, fragrant coffee for Anna and herself and put her headset back on. "Oh, honey, I hear you on that." She shook her head. "Must be a full moon tonight. I'm getting a lot of crazies, too."

Before Anna could complain further, her phone rang again. She muttered before answering it. "Please, God. Make it a nice one." Then she readied her polite, customer service voice, tapped her phone, and spoke into her mike. "Bethlehem Designs, this is Anna. How may I help you?"

"Hi, sweetie, this is Edith Melborn in New York. You want to bring up my account there? Zip code 10036—I know you need that."

"Thank you, Ms. Melborn, just one moment." Better. This lady had a gruff smoker's voice and a decided New York accent, but she sounded nice enough. So far, anyway. Anna typed away at her keyboard and raised her eyebrows when the account page opened on her computer screen.

"Wow, you live on Broadway, Ms. Melborn?" She caught herself too late. Some customers were uncomfortable with that kind of familiarity. "I mean, is that right? Do I have the right account open?"

She heard a chuckle. "That's right. Are you a fan of New York, dear?"

"Oh, it's my dream city. I just got my degree in theater. I mean, I got it last year." She glanced up at the photo pinned to her cubicle wall—fellow theater grads and her, embracing and laughing together on graduation day. The edges of the picture were worn. Too much time had passed since then, in Anna's opinion.

"So what are you doin' in Connecticut? You need to be up here for theater."

Easy for Ms. Moneybags to say. Anna eyed the woman's order history on the computer screen. A very big customer.

"One of these days, Ms. Melborn. I need to build up a bit of a nest egg before I do the starving-artist thing."

"Understood, understood. Well, you be sure to

come visit us soon. I'll be sure to have my son show you around. I need him to get away from the horrible woman he's seeing right now. Such a piece of work. You sound very sweet. So you let me know when you're ready to visit."

Anna saw the call timer on her phone's display. Her supervisor was a stickler for short sales calls.

"I will! I'll visit as soon as possible! And how can I help you today?"

"Right, well, I'm having an event up here next month or so. If you check my order history there, there are some monogrammed table linens you've done for me before, and I—"

Anna heard a swift, sharp intake of breath, as if Ms. Melborn had just been frightened by something.

"I'm sorry? Ms. Melborn?"

Dead silence.

"Ms. Mel—" She heard another strong gasp and then what sounded like frightened crying. Goosebumps rose on her arms, and she looked around the call center as if she might need someone else to handle the situation. She spoke loudly back into her headset.

"Ms. Melborn? Are you there? Are you all right?"

Now Cheryl turned and gave Anna her attention. She frowned with concern, even while she spoke to a customer on her own line.

A pained, distant voice whispered to Anna over the phone, one faint word at a time. Clearly Ms. Melborn no longer had the phone to her ear.

"Heart." Another stuttered gasp. "Attack."

Now Anna gasped. She stood abruptly from her chair, and the cord of her headset yanked her back down. It fell across her eyes and tangled in her long hair. She wrestled with it and ripped it away. She jolted upright. Again, she looked around the center as if someone else needed to handle this emergency. But there was no time for that. She grabbed her cell phone, tapped 9-1-1, and barked out orders as soon as she got an answer.

The operator was frustratingly calm. In fact, it wasn't clear she had understood what Anna said.

"9-1-1, repeat, please. What is your emergency?"

"Yeah, I need you to contact 9-1-1 in Manhattan! I'm here in Bethlehem on another phone line with a customer. She's in New York. She's having a heart attack. Please! Get help for her!"

"We can do that for you, ma'am. I know this is difficult, but I need you to calm down and answer a few questions."

Anna sat back down at her computer and told the operator Ms. Melborn's name, address, and telephone number. Her hair stuck to the moisture on her forehead and neck.

"But she won't be able to answer her phone, 'cause she's on this other phone with me. Or she was. I don't know if she's even conscious. I don't know if—"

She brought the headset back to her ear and spoke into her mike.

"Ms. Melborn? Can you hear me? Are you all right?"

Nothing.

Anna nearly yelled into the mike. "I'm getting help for you!"

When she pulled the headset away and picked up her cell, she could hear that the dispatcher had been talking to her.

"I'm sorry, what?"

At this point, several of Anna's co-workers stood around her desk, enthralled by what was unfolding.

The dispatcher spoke again. "I have police and ambulance on the way to Ms. Melborn. I need you to verify your own information as well, now."

Once Anna finished answering the dispatcher's questions, she hung up and nearly broke into tears.

Gary, her supervisor, had joined the onlookers. At his orders, Anna's co-workers slowly migrated back to their cubicles.

Cheryl put an arm around her and gave Gary a pointed look. "You need to take a break, Anna. That was rough."

"I don't know why I'm so upset." Anna wiped away a tear.

Cheryl tsked and rubbed her shoulder. "Don't be silly."

"I mean, of course it's horrible. But I don't know that lady from Adam, and I feel like it was my own relative or something. And I might never find out if she's all right or not. I won't know if I was able to, to get help to her in time." Her voice broke, and tears stung her eyes again.

Gary finally spoke to her. He checked his watch. "Look, you only have another half hour on your shift. Why don't you go ahead on home? And maybe we can check up on the customer in a few days. We have her contact information."

Anna nodded. But did she really need to leave early, or was she taking advantage of the circumstances? Then she imagined taking another call, trying to sound all upbeat and calm, and she decided going home was a good idea.

Halfway home she realized she had yet to turn on any music, which she always played during her commute. She turned on the classical station. Maybe it would be soothing. She'd been so distracted, she didn't even remember driving. Where had her attention been?

But she knew. She had been opening herself up to feelings of guilt. She had been thinking about poor Edith Melborn, a kind lady she had referred to as Ms. Moneybags. It wasn't *Edith's* fault she was wealthy. She was just trying to be nice to Anna, and Anna was all smart mouthed in response. In her head, yes, but still.

Was Edith with us? Or had her last moments been spent all alone, in agony? Had her last words—"heart attack"—been gritted out to a total stranger?

Lord, if Edith is alive, please ease her pain and help her get better. Does she know You? Does she have family? Friends? Her son—she mentioned her son. Will the hospital know to call him? Please have him go to her tonight. Please don't let her feel lonely. She was so nice to me. She had no idea what was coming.

Anna turned her music off and pressed the phone button on her steering wheel. She knew what she needed to do right now to feel a little bit better about the situation. She couldn't help Edith beyond prayer, but she knew what God was prompting her to do.

Her hands-free phone system asked for her input, and she breathed with a sense of relief before responding.

"Call Mom."

Chapter Two

Two days later Anna arrived at her work cubicle just as Cheryl finished a sales call.

"Welcome back, Miss Superhero." Cheryl's toothy grin was a great mood lifter. "I assume you took yesterday off to recoup from your customer's heart attack scare? A little rest in the gorgeous weather?"

Anna shook her head and logged into her computer. "Nope. I was already scheduled off, but that worked out perfectly. You're right, it was just beautiful yesterday, and I got a little Mom time in. That poor New York lady. She made me realize how precious family is, you know?"

Cheryl's phone rang before she could respond. As soon as Anna clocked in online, she sought out Gary. She found him in the kitchen, having an argument with the vending machine. Apparently the vending machine was winning.

"Hey, Gary. Did you happen to try to reach that customer in New York? The heart attack lady? I was just wondering if—"

He immediately stepped away from the machine, and his expression brightened. "You're going to love this. Her son called here this morning. She insisted he call us. And they were looking for *you*."

"So she's okay?" Again, Anna was amazed at how emotionally invested she felt with Ms. Melborn. "That's such a relief." She walked to the vending machine and gave it one practiced bang with the side of her fist. Gary's bag of pretzels obediently fell to the retrieval slot. "But why were they looking for me?"

"How do you *do* that?" Gary pulled the pretzels from the machine and didn't wait for an answer. "The woman thinks you're a miracle worker, from the sound of it. Said your quick thinking saved her life. Her doctor said the same thing, according to her son."

Anna smiled and got herself a cup of coffee. "Sounds like someone's due a raise. I mean, how many customer service reps are lifesavers, right?" She knew nothing of the sort would happen, but she couldn't resist the dig. She made so little here at Bethlehem Designs, she truly felt her wheels were spinning. It was going to be ages before she could save enough to go to New York.

"We'll put a big fat gold star in your file," Gary said. "So, listen, she's still in the hospital, but she asked if you would give her a call."

Anna knew her expression was puzzled now. "Seriously? Did she say why?"

Gary shook his head and popped a pretzel in his mouth. He spoke around it. "It wasn't her. It was her son. He says she wants you to call her. He gave me her cell number. We don't want to force you to become her best friend, but we'd appreciate it if you just gave her a few minutes of your time. I think she just wants to thank you herself. It will be good for business, and she gives us a *lot* of business."

Anna shrugged. "Sure. Give me her number, and I'll call her before I get on the service line. I'm glad she's all right."

~

She was surprised at how quickly Ms. Melborn answered the phone. She didn't sound quite as robust as the last time Anna spoke with her, but she also didn't sound as if she had just been near death.

"Oh, darling, how are you? Thanks for calling me. I just had to talk with you after you were so marvelous."

Darling? She was darling now? Ms. Melborn was a hoot.

"I'm so glad to know you're okay, Ms. Melborn. You really had me scared there."

The throaty chuckle in response made Anna smile.

"You said your name is Anna, right? Anna?"

"Yes, Ma'am."

"Well, Anna, you and me both. I was scared enough for the both of us, I'll tell you. Pain like you wouldn't believe. And the pressure. *Such* pressure. My doctor says you maybe saved my life, calling the medics like you did. You're a gem, dear. A total gem."

"It was my pleasure, Ms. Melborn."

"Fine, well, now it's my pleasure. I want to pay you back for caring enough to do what you did."

Anna didn't respond right away. What do you say to that? She had to admit, the idea of a little extra money was tempting. "But, that's not necessary, Ms. Melborn. Anyone would have called 9-1-1 for you, I'm sure."

"We both know that's not the case, Anna. Here's what I'd like to do. Don't think I wasn't listening before. You got your degree in theater. You want to come to New York. Well, I want to make that happen. For a while, anyway. I want you to take some time off from that job, which I'm sure you hate, and come to New York for . . . for six months. We'll start with that."

Anna broke out in a sweat. This woman was constantly making her sweat.

"I'll foot the bill," Ms. Melborn said. "I have an apartment you can use. I'll give you an expense account. And I have a few connections with theater people. You saved my life, darling girl. Maybe I can save yours in return."

Anna wondered if maybe *she* would have a heart attack. "I, Ms. Melborn, I don't know what to say. Are you serious? But, I mean, I don't know if I could take that much time off of work—"

More chuckling. "Right. You wouldn't want to jeopardize such a terrific career there in customer service, would you? Are you less hungry for the theater than I thought?"

Anna opened and shut her mouth, frowning. This lady was sharp. "Uh, no. I'm as hungry as you thought. I mean, I think I am. Or, I *am* hungry, I just don't know how hungry you thought I was."

She sensed Cheryl turning in her chair to study her. Anna realized she sounded like an idiot.

"There you go, dear," Ms. Melborn said. "You go ahead and talk to your boss there, and I'll make some arrangements here. We'll be in touch. You call me if you need to, or my son, Paul, will call you. Paul handles most of my business affairs."

Is that what Anna was going to be? One of wealthy Ms. Melborn's business affairs? She wasn't sure she liked that, but she wasn't sure she didn't, either. She needed to think. She didn't want to log onto the call line and start taking orders for personalized linens, that's for sure.

"Okay, Ms. Melborn. I'll call back. And thank you. I'm…a little floored by your offer, I have to admit."

"Good. I like to have that effect on people. Later, dear."

~

And so it was, three weeks later, that Anna's flight landed at LaGuardia Airport precisely on schedule, and she headed to the baggage claim.

Was she insane? What was she walking into? Or flying into? Ms. Melborn was obviously a financially successful woman who had, as she claimed, some contacts in the theater world. But that was almost all she knew about her. Anna had done what little Internet sleuthing she could, but there wasn't much information online.

Still, she knew such an opportunity would not likely come along again. Everyone had encouraged her to take this trip—her parents, her sister, her hometown friends, her college friends, her co-workers. Even her boss urged her to accept Ms. Melborn's offer.

"I can't guarantee you a job if things don't work out," Gary said, "but if it were me, I'd go in a second. If nothing else, you'll probably have a great time up there."

The logistics had freaked her out. She wasn't about to give up her apartment, because who knew what her circumstances would be in six months? But her younger sister, Diane, loved the idea of subletting the place from her at a lowered rate. Anna didn't know how to pack for a six-month stay—too long for a single suitcase, but too short for a full-on shipment of all of her possessions.

"You take a couple suitcases with you," her mother said. "And, if necessary, we can box up some of your things and send them on once you have a better idea of what you need."

"Thanks, Mom. I swear, I don't think I could even make this move without all the help and advice from everyone. Makes me feel so immature."

Her mother laughed. "You're only twenty-three, honey. This is a big deal. But it will be great. You have a fairy godmother helping out, and not many young actresses have that."

Anna tilted her head. "I just, I mean, I know as a so-called creative type I should have a more carefree attitude about this, this adventure, I guess you could call it. But you know me, Mom. I like to be in control as much as possible. Ms. Melborn is giving me a terrific career opportunity, but she's also making me really uncomfortable about my immediate future."

"Maybe that discomfort is a good thing," her mother said. "*You're* not in control, remember? Have you prayed about the trip?"

"Of course. And I know God's in control. But you know I like to wrestle it from Him once in a while. He seems to understand."

~

And now, as she waited for her luggage to arrive on the conveyor belt, she struggled with turning over that control again.

Lord, I'm downright scared at the moment. Of course, You know that already. I do appreciate this blessing, though. And I ask that You help me to make good decisions. Please help me to stay focused on Your guidance. If I'm here to walk a path You've set out for me, please help me to keep from being distracted by anything or anyone not in Your plan.

Someone cleared his throat behind her, and she turned around to face a well-dressed young guy with short dark hair and fashionable scruff on his face.

"Are you Anna, by any chance?"

"Uh, yes. Anna Chesterfield." She jutted her hand forward like a robot. He actually jerked back ever so slightly before smiling and shaking her hand. His hand was warm, and his blue eyes were kind.

"Paul Melborn. Edith's son."

Anna had expected an older man. Edith sounded pretty old on the phone, so Anna pictured her son as more than middle aged. This man wasn't a day over thirty, if that. And she realized he was speaking to her while she stared blankly into his crystal clear eyes.

"I'm sorry," she said. "I blanked out there for a

minute. What did you say?"

He smiled again. "Nothing important. Just 'welcome to New York' and that kind of thing. Let's get your bags. I have a car just outside."

He looked at the conveyor belt and she made note of his excellent jawline. But this time, when he looked back at her, she was ready. She spotted one of her bags and pointed at it as she approached it. "There's one."

Still, she had already started praying again. If anything or anyone was going to be distracting on this trip, it was the friendly young man standing at her side.

Chapter Three

Edith was, indeed, younger than Anna had imagined. She was in her late fifties or early sixties, and she was in a fire-red tracksuit when Paul ushered Anna into Edith's spacious apartment.

She came around the corner and went straight for Anna. She was in full makeup, her blond-gray hair was in a "do," and her hug was perfumey and brief.

"I'm all sweaty from the stationary bike. Don't want to get you messy. The doctors, you know. Got to keep the heart going. And make up for all those years of smoking. Why did you bring her bags up here, Paul?"

Ah, good. Anna had been concerned that she was supposed to stay in Edith's home. She wouldn't have uttered a word of complaint, but she would have found the arrangement awkward.

"Just thought you two would like to meet right away. I'll bring you downstairs now, Anna." He laughed at himself. "I guess that was kind of bad planning on my part."

Edith gave him a motherly pat on the cheek. "Not at all, sweetheart. We'll all go down together."

They rode the elevator to the second floor. Even though the apartment was considerably smaller than Edith's, it was the fanciest place Anna had ever lived in.

"This was where we lived when the kids were younger. We've never sold it since. Paul's big sister, Rachel, lived here before she married. And now you. For a while, anyway, right? I hope you don't mind that I use the two small bedrooms for storage. The master is good sized. And I had the cleaning service freshen up the place so it wouldn't have that closed-up smell places get. It's nice, right?"

Anna followed Edith and Paul as they showed her around the apartment. "This is absolutely gorgeous, Ms. Melborn."

"Edith, dear. You should call me Edith now."

Anna nodded. "Edith. You're too generous."

Edith approached her and held Anna's face in her hands. "And you're a good girl. Isn't she a good girl, Paul? What a doll you are! Pretty as can be. Isn't she pretty, Paul?"

Anna cringed and was too embarrassed to look at Paul after Edith released her face. She heard a fond chuckle come from him.

"Yes. A good girl, a doll, and very pretty."

Anna looked at him then. His expression showed he understood her discomfort, and she immediately relaxed. But her cheeks still burned.

The two of them had spoken little on the drive from LaGuardia. Although he apologized for being inattentive, Paul had received one business call after another. One comment he had made, though, was that his mother wasn't the type to waste time. And now Edith proved that.

"So. Anna. You take a couple hours to settle in, unpack, freshen up, and then you and I are going to have dinner with an agent friend of mine. You want to join us, Paul?"

"Thanks, Mom, no. I have plans." He carried Anna's luggage into the master bedroom.

Edith took the opportunity to mutter to Anna. "Probably that awful girlfriend of his I told you about. Ugh. Such a nightmare, that woman."

Paul returned and shook Anna's hand. "Pleasure, Anna. I'll be seeing you here and there, I'm sure."

"More than that," Edith said. "I want you to chauffeur her around until she gets her bearings, and don't tell me you don't have time for that. I know how much business you do in that car."

He looked like he was about to argue, but he got that same fond look in his eyes, nearly rolling them. "That will probably be fine. We'll work it out."

When Edith wasn't looking, Anna winced at

him and mouthed "Sorry!" He subtly shook his head to dismiss her concern. He gave her a quick smile, and she felt like a schoolgirl for the little flip in her stomach. Ridiculous.

"Come on, Mom, I'll ride back up with you before I head out." He opened the door and gently placed his hand on his mother's back.

"All right, Anna, so come on up at six," Edith said over her shoulder, "and we'll go meet with Gretchen. Nothing too fancy, just some nice slacks and a blouse, something like that. It's hot, but we'll be in air conditioning." Edith gave Paul an adoring look. "You're a good boy. A good man."

He smiled as if he heard that often. And as if she were someone he wanted to protect.

Anna looked at the closed door for a moment. Yes, from the looks of it, a very good man.

~

Not only did Gretchen, the agent, take an immediate liking to Anna, she handed her a script at dinner that evening and told her she had one day to prepare for her first audition.

"You'll read for Lucinda. Just pages ten through twenty or so, the CD says," Gretchen said. "That stands for Casting Director."

Anna nodded. "Yes." She knew that. But one day to prepare? She hoped Edith didn't have anything else planned for her before the audition. "I'll be ready."

~

And she was. She spent all day preparing the section Gretchen pointed out, and she read through the rest of the play several times. It wasn't a huge part, but it was a speaking part, which was an amazing gift. She knew Lucinda's lines perfectly on pages nine through twenty-two, just to play it safe.

She had to force herself to sleep that night, and she was still wired when Paul arrived in the morning to drive her to the theater.

She kept her layered, light-brown hair loose and wore a slim, belted dress and heels, because that was the way she pictured Lucinda. And maybe Gretchen had suggested something similar. Anna wasn't certain, because it was all happening so quickly, and she wasn't completely on top of things. She had just been a customer service rep a few weeks ago, and now she was about to audition for a New York play. Her stomach clenched tighter than a fist.

"You look great." Paul opened the car door for her. "Nervous?"

She blew a piece of hair away from her eyes and gave him a helpless look. "How can you tell?"

"I just don't think I've ever seen anyone bite away their lipstick that quickly."

She gasped and flipped the visor mirror down. "You're right!" She frantically rifled through her purse to get her lip gloss back out. "This casting director is going to turn me away before I utter a word."

Paul pulled out into traffic. "Listen, Gretchen is going to send you on a number of auditions while you're here. You've only been here two days. Don't feel like this is your only shot."

"Maybe so, but I've just never done anything so . . . big before. I can't seem to get my heart to stop hammering."

"What do you usually do to calm your nerves?"

She took a deep breath. Moment of truth here. "I pray."

He nodded, his eyes on the traffic. "Same here."

"Really?" She didn't mean to sound as surprised as she did.

He laughed. "Should I be insulted? Don't I seem like the praying type?"

"Oh. Sorry. You, uh, don't seem like the type to get nervous."

He cut her an amused glance. "You're not lying about praying, are you, Anna?"

"Seriously. You seem unflappable. But that is *not* me. I'm very flappable. Especially right now, so don't get me more flustered than I already am."

"All right. I'll keep silent and give you a chance to pray, how about that? And I'll pray for you, too."

~

As it turned out, Anna needed a church-load of prayer. The moment she stepped on the cavernous, empty stage, the CD threw her off kilter.

"All right, let's have you read for Bertie. Page 30, halfway down. When you're ready."

Bertie? Wait, *Bertie*?

"I thought I was reading for Lucinda."

In the dimly lit seats, the CD shook her head. "Yeah, but you're not right for Lucinda. Lucinda is voluptuous, and that ain't you. We'll try you for Bertie."

She had barely noticed Bertie as she read through the script before. She wondered if the sweat that worked its way throughout her dress was visible from the seats.

~

Paul took her for coffee when she slogged out of the theater. "I'm telling you," he said, "don't let it get to you. There will be other opportunities."

"Ugh." She pulled the damp bodice of her dress away from her chest. "I was like a plaster mannequin up there. A plaster mannequin who hadn't bothered to prepare. So embarrassing."

"They've seen worse, I'm sure. Shrug it off. Gretchen will have something else for you. Have you checked in with her yet?"

"No. I'm dreading it." She stared at her coffee and imagined how she must have seemed on that stage, reading from the page and failing to project the simplest appropriate tone to match the words she read.

"Call her," Paul said. "She's on your side. We all are."

She looked up at him. "What? I'm sorry, I was busy mentally beating my self-esteem to a pulp. What did you say?" She had heard him a little, but she wanted to listen with enough attention to truly savor his kindness.

His grin was quick. "We're all on your side. We all want you to do well. To move up here and eventually consider New York your home."

She sighed, puzzled. "Why are you being so nice to me? I just don't get it."

He leaned toward her across the table. How ice-clear blue eyes could reflect such warmth, she did not know.

"I act like my mother is a little demanding, and she is, sometimes. But I'm not at all ashamed to say I love her to death. I don't know if you're aware of how much I appreciate you for helping her when she was helpless. You saved her life. I want to do what I can—as my mother does—to help you get what you want."

She smiled, and he sat back. Despite what he said, he looked a little embarrassed for having been so dramatic.

"Besides," he said, "I think I like you. Just in general."

Anna couldn't look away from those eyes. "I think I like you, too. In general."

Her phone vibrated and they both looked at it. Anna took a deep breath when she read the screen. "Gretchen. Guess it's time to face the news."

But Paul had managed to encourage her. In fact, he had managed to do more than that. She had to remind herself that he had a girlfriend. A horrible nightmare of a girlfriend.

She needed to refresh her sense of purpose here. Gretchen would slap some sense into her, she was sure.

Chapter Four

Gretchen did slap her, in a sense.

"Yeah, Marla said you were awful, but don't worry about that. She didn't tell us what she wanted, so that's on her."

Awful? She knew she had been bad, but ouch.

"Don't you worry, though. You're here for at least six months, as far as Edith is concerned. You know how great that is?"

"Yes, I do. I—"

"I'm going to send you on plenty of auditions. But what I think you should do, now that we have a little time until the next one, is come on over to my office and let me watch you. Act, I mean. I want to see what I'm talking-up here. You have time right now?"

Anna looked at Paul, who was texting someone. "Uh, Paul, do you have time to drop me off at Gretchen's office?"

He sent his text, finished off his coffee, and

stood. "Yep. Let's go."

~

Anna appreciated that Gretchen was as frank as she was. It made it easier to believe her when she praised Anna's skills.

"Marla's way off base," Gretchen said. "She should have let you read for Lucy. That reading was beautiful, Anna. Really beautiful. I'll be happy to send you to every audition that fits."

And Gretchen did exactly that. Over the following four months, Anna prepared and auditioned for eleven different roles. Still, nothing produced an offer.

When she saw Paul waiting for her outside her eleventh attempt, she cringed at the thought of telling him once again that she'd been turned down. Here it was, a sunny but refreshingly brisk October afternoon, and she felt like gloom personified. She wished the casting directors would all deal specifically with Gretchen, but this one today was decidedly against her for the part and swiftly told her so.

But as she reached the car, the CD's assistant ran out to stop her.

"They want you to come back and read again," he said, panting from his run.

Anna looked at Paul, who raised his eyebrows and flicked his hand at her as if he were shooing her toward the theater.

"Get back in there, young lady. Second chances and all that. Knock 'em dead."

She frowned, even as she turned back again. She muttered to herself as she followed the assistant back into the theater. "I didn't knock 'em at *all* the first time."

"Huh?" The assistant looked over his shoulder at her.

"Oh, nothing. I'm just surprised she wants me to read again."

"Yeah, it's not her. It's the director."

Anna caught her breath. "Did the director see my audition?"

"Guess so." He pointed toward the stage. "He's the old guy in the corduroy jacket."

Stan Leopold, Gretchen had said. He sat with the CD in the red velvet audience chairs and turned toward Anna as she approached. She saw his eyes light up.

He enveloped her right hand with both of his. He had a loud, sharp-edged voice. "Anna. Thanks for coming back. Anna, right?"

"Yes, sir. Anna Chesterfield."

The casting director wouldn't look at her, but Leopold acted as if everything was fine.

"All right, Anna Chesterfield. I'm Stan. I'm directing this play, assuming everything falls into place. And I liked what I saw a moment ago."

Did she just hear the casting director snort?

Stan took Anna's hand and looped her arm through his, as if they were going to the prom together. He walked her back to the stage steps. "You go on back up there and let us see you again. And walk around a little."

She had the forethought, as she usually did right before an audition, to send out a quick prayer.

Please help me relax, Lord. And if it's Your will, please give me this part!

As nervous as she was to audition in front of Stan, she experienced a double dose of confidence from praying and from knowing he had asked for her to return. She could tell she gave a strong performance this time.

Still, a hushed argument ensued between Stan and the CD. Anna wasn't quite sure what she was supposed to do. Finally, Stan put up his hand.

"Right, Anna. Excellent. We'll get back to your agent. Again, thanks for coming back in."

"Yes, sir."

Still no eye contact from the casting director as Anna descended the steps. Obviously she hadn't wowed *everyone*.

But the last thing she noticed was that the director kept his eyes on her as she passed them. "Give Edith my love," he said with a wink.

~

Anna walked toward the car before fully noticing that Paul was talking with a stunning young woman straight off the cover of *Vogue*. Or, rather, the woman was talking to Paul. And pointing her finger at him. And jutting her chin at him.

Anna slowed down. This wasn't a conversation she wanted to interrupt.

But Paul glanced her way, which prompted the woman to look at her, as well.

Although she was as beautiful as Anna first thought, head on she looked like a young Cruella de Vil, white hair streak and all. "I suppose this is *her*." Much drama poured out with the accusation.

Paul spoke calmly and politely, but his frustration was obvious. "Hi, Anna. I'd like you to meet Tara—"

"His *girlfriend*." The words were nearly spat in Anna's face.

Still, her customer service behavior kicked in, and she spoke as if everything were perfectly fine. She put out her hand. "So nice to meet you, Tara."

Tara ignored the gesture. "Yeah, a real thrill." She glared at Paul. "I know your dear mother is forcing you to do this, Paul, but just know I won't wait around forever for you to finish chauffeuring little Miss Suburbia here. I need to have a life, too."

She shot an all-encompassing glance of disgust at Anna and walked away from them. As angry as she was, she did that exaggerated, runway pony-prance of a walk models do, as if she assumed everyone were watching her.

That last little jab about Edith forcing Paul to spend time with Anna was a bit more painful than she liked. She met eyes with Paul and gave him a fake smile. "Now, Paul, why haven't I met that ray of sunshine before?"

His frown vanished and he looked at the ground, chuckling. "I'm so sorry. I'd like to say Tara is usually a lot more pleasant. But the truth is, she's only gotten worse. I told her last night we should stop seeing each other. She knew my schedule for today, and I guess she decided to stage this little scene for your benefit. Please don't take her insults to heart. She's just angry—"

"*Is* she? How can you tell?"

Anna's phone rang before he could answer. "It's Gretchen. Hang on, Paul."

"Victory, sweetie!" Gretchen nearly shouted. "Stan loves you! You've got the part!"

Anna stared at Paul while Gretchen gave her details about upcoming table reads and rehearsals. Those details would have to be repeated, because all Anna could do was flash a wide-eyed smile at Paul that prompted one on his part as well. He raised his eyebrows, clearly asking if she had good news. When she nodded, he swooped her into a hug before she had a chance to react.

"Are you hearing me, Anna?" Gretchen's voice cut through their hushed laughter. "I'll have a contract for you soon. Stan wants to get moving, and you were the last piece of the puzzle."

Anna pulled away from Paul, and the embarrassed look in his eyes mirrored how she felt. She had enjoyed that hug a little too much.

"I, I didn't hear you on all of the details, Gretchen, sorry. Are there dates I need to make note of?"

"Not really, not yet. I'll get back to you in the next day or so. But congratulations! Edith is so happy for you, too."

Anna couldn't help but frown. "Edith? She knows already?"

A moment's pause. "Oh, right. Well, I was on the phone with Edith when Stan's call came through. So she couldn't wait for me to call back. She pestered me by text while Stan and I were on the phone." Gretchen chuckled. "You've made such an impression on her. She loves you like a daughter."

When her call from Gretchen ended, Paul immediately spoke. "I'm going to take you to a celebratory lunch. If you're free, that is."

Anna pretended to consult the calendar on her phone. "Hmm, I don't know. Let me see. It looks like I'm open from now 'til . . . forever."

Paul shook his head. "Not anymore! Pretty soon you're going to be too busy to spend any time with me—with anyone, I mean. You have to let me celebrate with you before you become a famous

Broadway star."

Anna released a theatrical sigh. "Ah, the little people. One has to save time for the little people."

"There ya go." Paul put out his arm and escorted her to the car.

She couldn't help asking, once they drove away from the theater. "Paul, is your mother powerful enough to force a director to hire me?"

"What? No! No New York director is going to put his play on the line like that. You earned that part, Anna. Enjoy your accomplishment. Really. That was all you."

He was genuine. So was Edith. They had both been nothing but kind and welcoming to her during this entire process.

So what was it? Why did she have an unshakeable concern in the back of her mind about this play?

Chapter Five

Once Anna had her rehearsal schedule from Gretchen, Paul drew her a little deeper into the Melborn family.

"Come with me to Long Island this weekend. I'm visiting my sister and her family, and they'd love to meet you. Mom keeps telling them how great you are."

Anna wasn't about to argue with three such agreeable sentences in a row. "They won't mind? Do they have room for me?"

Paul gave her a wry smile. "This is Long Island we're talking about. Rachel and Mike will never have enough kids to fill all the bedrooms in that ridiculous house of theirs. Besides, Rachel specifically asked me to invite you."

"And your Mom? She doesn't want to go?"

"She has that charity dinner thing she called you about at your Connecticut company last month. The one she needed the linens for? She and some of her ladies are having a blast putting the event together.

That's one area she doesn't need my help in, and I thank God for that every day."

~

They hadn't gone far on their drive to Long Island before Anna tiptoed onto a subject that had been teasing at her since the day she got her part in the play.

"Um, Paul? You know when your—when Tara said that stuff in front of the theater?"

He tilted his head and looked as chagrined as if it had just happened. "Yeah, again, I'm sorry about that. You didn't deserve that."

"No, that's not why I brought it up. I'm fine. But you said the whole scene was probably something she did for my benefit."

"Mm hmm."

"Why me?" Anna asked. "Why my benefit?"

He opened his mouth to speak and then shut it again. "Oh. Right."

She was surprised to see him blush. He always seemed far too cool to get embarrassed to that degree.

"Well, I might have unwittingly said something to make her think…well, that I was a little too impressed with you."

Now Anna felt a flush of her own. She had to admit she would have been flattered had he said something about finding her attractive, but to be impressed with her? She didn't think anyone had ever been terribly impressed by her. She loved the fact that what he liked had nothing to do with her looks.

Paul continued. "I mean, I spoke about you as I would have about any *man* who was as quick-thinking and considerate as you were when Mom needed help. And I would have commended any *guy* who would take the chance to come up here and trust two relative strangers with his immediate future the way you trusted Mom and me."

"Take a chance?" Anna scoffed. "Edith is totally footing my bill and getting me auditions I could never have gotten on my own. And you're devoting *so* much of your time to help me get around New York. I don't know many people who wouldn't have jumped at the chance you two are giving me."

"Thanks. That might be what Tara disliked to begin with—our obvious fondness for you. But I think she lost it a little out there in front of the theater when she saw that you were so…"

She just waited for him to finish that sentence.

"Well, you have a really sweet air about you, Anna. And you're, I mean, I would imagine Tara thought you were… very pretty."

He shifted in his seat and adjusted the rear-view mirror.

Anna couldn't help it. She smiled. She appreciated that he talked about being impressed with her and being fond of her. But she had to admit it. She liked that he thought she was pretty.

He glanced her way and caught her smiling. A wonderful sense of comfort settled upon her when he gave her a pure, natural smile in return.

~

"Ah, the famous Anna!" Paul's brother-in-law, Mike, enveloped Anna in a warm hug before she even walked through the door. "Rachel's dying to meet you." He turned and started to call out to Rachel, but she walked briskly toward Anna and Paul, carrying a cherub of a girl in her arms.

"BeeBee! There's my girl!" Paul grabbed the little girl and spun her around before burying his face in her neck, provoking unrestrained giggling from her. In an effort to make him stop, she pounded on him with the stuffed bunny in her hands.

Rachel embraced Anna and led her into their massive home. "Oh, welcome! Thank you for coming on such short notice, Anna. And congrats on the part in the play! Mom is crazy proud of you."

The moment Paul and Mike turned their backs, Rachel whispered to Anna. "And I'm afraid Mom has decided to play matchmaker, now that the dreaded Tara has finally moved on to torment some other poor schlub. I think Mom believes Paul finally ended that mess because of you."

Anna was overwhelmed by the quickness of Rachel's disclosure. She just widened her eyes and stuttered. "Uh, really?"

Mike called over his shoulder, "Rachel! Leave the poor woman alone." He shook his head at Paul. "These Melborn women are impossible romantics." Over his shoulder he said, "And notorious busybodies!"

Rachel looked at Anna and rolled her eyes. "Ignore him. And me. I'm just glad to have you visit." Again, she lowered her voice. "Paul speaks very highly of you."

Anna laughed. Mike was right. Impossibly romantic and nosy.

~

Rachel and Mike were clearly at least as well off financially as were Edith and Paul. Their home was gorgeous and beautifully situated near the shore, and every room looked like a feature from a home décor magazine. Still, they were some of the most down-to-earth, comfortable people Anna had ever met. When they all bowed their heads before dinner, Anna learned that they were a Christian family, and she secretly had to add to the dinner prayer a request that she would keep a clear head about herself. She knew that just because someone was a Christian didn't mean he was the man the Lord had in mind for you.

And on the heels of that prayer, she chided herself for even thinking that way so early into her relationship with Paul.

And on the heels of *that* thought, she wondered at her characterizing what she and Paul had as a "relationship." Whoa, girl.

They took a walk after dinner, she and Paul. The breeze off the water was brisk, and although Anna wore a thick cardigan, she realized she was underdressed. Paul must have noticed the shiver that ran through her. When they walked out onto the small dock, he took off his jacket and draped it across her shoulders.

"You okay with that?" He didn't release the jacket without her approval.

She smiled at him. "Thanks."

"Look at that sunset," Paul said. "Intoxicating. It's one of my favorite things about coming out here. The sunset over the water. Huge skies. No skyscrapers in the way."

"Do you ever think of moving out of Manhattan?" Anna pulled his jacket around herself. His fragrance wafted up from inside—whether it was cologne or his natural scent, she didn't know, but she loved it.

Paul shrugged and shoved his hands into the pockets of his jeans. "I don't think so, but you never know. I definitely won't leave Manhattan as long as Mom needs me." He chuckled. "I guess I sound like a mama's boy, huh? That was something Tara accused me of."

Wow, that Tara was one choice specimen.

"Not at all," Anna said. "If my dad goes before my mother, I know my sister and I will focus on her needs above all others. It's only right."

Paul nodded. "They were quite a duo, my parents. They had their fights, like any other couple, but what a united front they were. She was devastated when he died. We all were. I really miss him."

"How long ago?"

"Six years." He didn't hesitate at all, had the number right at the forefront. "It was unexpected. He was only in his early seventies, you know? Afterward, I always thought it was a blessing that God drew me toward an MBA instead of anything else I was considering. It made it easier to take over his responsibilities with their various businesses."

She studied his profile as he looked out at the horizon. "If you didn't have your responsibilities, is there something else you'd do?"

He smiled and looked at her. "I love music. I'd probably pursue something in that industry."

"Do you play an instrument?"

He shrugged. "A little guitar."

"Like a ukulele?" She smirked at him.

"That's me. Tiny bubbles. Tiny Tim. No, I'm a wannabe John Meyer, I guess. I still play when I have free time."

"I want to hear."

"It's a date, then. When we get back to

Manhattan."

After a comfortable silence, she said, "You getting cold?"

"Freezing!" He said it abruptly and with gritted teeth, and they both laughed.

They returned to the house, and before they entered, Anna began to remove his jacket from her shoulders. He went to help her, and they found themselves in an awkward tangle of arms that brought them both to self-deprecating laughter.

But Paul didn't remove his arms from around her shoulders, and the one natural place for her to put her arms seemed to be around him, as well. Their smiles had barely relaxed before he paused, leaned toward her, and gave her a gentle kiss on the lips.

He drew back and gave a soft whistle, cocking his head toward the horizon. "As I said. Intoxicating sunset."

She gave the tiniest nod. "Mm hmm." She walked into the house ahead of him, floating on a cloud and wondering if *this* was the behavior of a woman keeping a clear head.

Chapter Six

Anna joined her fellow cast mates around the reading table at the theater the following Monday. Her weekend with Paul and his sister's family had been quick and so much fun. It was sad to see it end.

Although she and Paul had clearly taken a few steps away from mere friendship toward something potentially more serious, they didn't really know that much about each other yet. She knew she found him more and more attractive the better she knew him. His eyes and rugged features were easy to appreciate, but what she liked more was the way he clearly loved and respected his mother and sister. She saw his protective nature with them, but he also gave both of them room to show their own capabilities. Anna didn't have a brother of her own, but that was the way her father treated her. So her comfort level with Paul was becoming strong.

But it was now time to get down to business, and her fingers and toes tingled with excitement.

Her first professional table read!

She struggled to keep her breathing calm until she realized there were two other actors at the table for whom this play was a professional first. Both guys. Relatively minor roles, like hers. She was grateful the three of them were invited to the table read, since many producers would just have an assistant read their lines.

"All right, let's get started, people." Stan flipped his chair around, sat down, and leaned against the chair back. "I haven't met all of you, but I'm Stan Leopold. I'm directing this masterpiece." He smiled at everyone at the table. Even though he had given Anna considerable attention when he called her back to audition last week, he didn't remember her name when they went through their initial introductions today. She clearly was in no danger of getting a swelled head.

"Many of you already know our producer, Phil Witowsky," Stan said. "And David here, Dave Milnes, he's our writer. So let's get a feel for his work and how it sounds outside his head." He pointed to the producer. "Phil, you're up."

The producer gave them a pep talk about running a tight, efficient, yet creative ship before he handed the reins back to Stan. It was clear Phil had the last word on every facet of the play, even though Stan would be the face of the play for the actors.

Stan put them through their paces, and for the most part, everyone read as if they were auditioning all over again. Especially Anna.

"You know they can replace any one of us at this point," Johnny, one of the other new actors, told her when they first arrived. "If they decide they made a mistake and you're not right for the part after all, it's sayonara, babe."

Anna harrumphed. "Thanks a lot. I needed a little extra nervousness for the day."

"Better to know now and do your best, right?"

He was right. So when her few moments came up, Anna gave her all. After her longest reading in the play, she caught Stan watching her. He looked pleased with her, even giving her a wink again.

"All right, let's break for a couple hours," he announced when they came to the end of the read. "We're going to do a bit of adjusting, and we want you back for a cold read on the changes, say four o'clock. Don't be late."

"Anna, come get lunch with us." The new actors and two of the more seasoned actresses started out together. She joined them, and they all walked down the street to the deli. The food in New York was one of Anna's favorite reasons for living here.

"So this is your first New York gig?" One of the women, Tess, sounded as hard boiled as her character was. And she ate her Reuben as if she had grown up with a brood of hungry brothers. But there was something Anna really liked about her. She liked her frankness, which they had all seen at the table read.

"Yeah. I can't quite believe it," Anna said. "Getting this job has been a real blessing."

"A blessing, huh?" Tess said. She chuckled. "I guess that's one way of looking at it."

"Why? How do you look at it? You don't believe in blessings?"

Tess shrugged. "I'm kind of a 'luck' girl, myself. I believe in the power of luck and—" she gave Anna a barely discernable once over "… and other things."

"Watch it, Tess." The other seasoned actress, Rhonna, shot a look of warning at Tess. "Don't start rumors. We don't need problems already."

"What rumors? What do you mean?" Anna didn't want to get into a gossip fest, but it did sound as if Tess wanted to give her a friendly warning.

Tess shook her head. "Don't listen to me. I'm a cynic." She pushed her plate toward Anna. "Have some chips, girl. You eat like a bird."

The conversation quickly veered away to other topics, but Anna couldn't fully engage at first. The last thing she wanted to become was a cynic. But neither did she want to be naïve.

She understood that Tess's comment was related to Anna's indirect reference to God and His blessings. A lot of people considered believers to be stupid and ignorant of the world. Anna had to admit she *was* a little ignorant of what life in New York City and the theater would be like. It was the kind of environment you could read all about but still not truly know until you lived in it.

But she did believe God brought her this opportunity, so by the time they returned to the theater she had given her worry over to Him.

Her lines hadn't been changed at all, but the main actors had quite a bit to work over.

"Fine by me, staying here longer," Johnny whispered during a quick break. "We get paid whether we're working or just watching. They'll probably send us home soon, though, for that very reason."

And they did end the session without completing a full read-through.

"All right, that's enough for the night, everybody." David, the writer, stood. "That's all we've changed, so you can all go home and study. Back first thing in the a.m. You like those changes okay, Stan?"

"Yep. They're great. 'Night, everyone."

Anna had almost forgotten about Stan. He didn't sit with them when they returned from lunch. But now he approached them as the actors filtered out.

She just gave him a nod as she followed the other actors.

He raised his index finger. "Hang on a second,

Anna. Bring me your script here, if you don't mind, dear."

Oh no. Was this what Johnny had mentioned in the morning? Had she already managed to lose the job before they really got underway?

Stan walked back toward the theater seats, where he sat during their afternoon read-through. She followed, praying all the while.

Please, Lord, help me calm down and trust You in this. Please don't let him fire me!

"Have a seat, Anna." He sat and lowered the cushioned seat next to his until she finished lowering it herself. As she sat, she didn't turn toward him quite as freely as he turned toward her.

"You like the part?" His voice was kind.

She smiled, but she knew the smile was stiff, full of fear.

She was an actress, for goodness' sake. She needed to act as if she felt confident.

"I love it! Thank you so much for giving me a chance." If he took that chance away, she had to take it well. She had to stay professional.

She readied herself.

"Good. Would you mind reading that part in the third act? The longer one?"

Read? Again? *Oh, Lord, please don't let him fire me!*

"Sure." She closed her eyes to place herself in the scene and the mood. Then she read as if everything depended on her performance. She forgot all about Stan sitting there.

He softly clapped his hands for her when she finished, and he smiled broadly. When he stopped clapping, he patted her knee. "Excellent, dear. Excellent."

The pat shook her, but she tried not to look askance at his hand. When he stopped patting and just left his hand on her knee, she couldn't help it. She looked at his hand as if it were radioactive.

And when his hand remained, she forced herself to look him in the eye. He was still smiling at her, without a hint of lasciviousness. He could have been her old Uncle Charlie, encouraging her to learn to ride a bike when she was five, or congratulating her for winning the 60-meter dash in elementary school.

But he wasn't her old Uncle Charlie, and she wasn't a child. Or an idiot.

She slowly stood and pasted on that polite smile again.

"I should probably go, if that's all right, Mr. Leopold."

"Call me Stan." He remained in his seat and acted as if nothing had happened.

She nodded. "Stan. My boyfriend is waiting to drive me home." She prayed he didn't know there was no boyfriend.

"Sure. We'll see you tomorrow then. Study your

lines. Get some rest. Good job today."

She felt as if he watched her all the way out of the theater. She would wait until she got outside, around other people, before texting Paul to see if he could pick her up.

Tess's lunchtime comment came to mind. Now it made sense.

Here she was afraid Stan was going to fire her, and now she was very likely going to have to quit.

Chapter Seven

Paul looked at Anna a little longer than usual when she got in the car. "You look a little tired. Rough read today?" He pulled away from the curb, but he glanced at her again.

She shook her head. She wasn't tired at all. Maybe Paul couldn't decipher her moods yet because they didn't know each other terribly well.

"Not tired, no. Maybe a little upset. Shocked, even."

He frowned, clearly concerned. That was more the reaction Anna expected.

"What's wrong?" he asked. "What happened? You all right?"

Yes, a much better reaction.

"Um, I think Stan—the director—I think he just came on to me."

She expected him to look as shocked as she felt. Maybe even outraged. But he surprised her.

"You *think* he did? What did he do?" He asked with total calm. He wasn't shocked at all.

"He had me stay after everyone else left. He

asked me to read a monologue, and then he patted my knee and told me I did well."

The amusement in Paul's eyes was downright condescending. "And?"

"And he left it there."

"Left what where?"

"His hand! He left it on my knee!" What was the matter with him? Was he deliberately struggling to picture the moment? "He kept it right there, and I don't know what he planned to do after that." She huffed.

Paul nodded. Anna could see he understood his response wasn't ideal. "Well…what *did* he do after that?"

"Nothing! Because I stood up. I didn't want to stick around to see what else he had in mind."

And again with the nodding. Eyes on the road. Nodding as if she had given him directions to take a left up ahead.

Did she expect Paul to turn the car around, run it up onto the curb in heated anger, jump out of the car, and go pummel Stan for what he did to her?

Hmm. Maybe. Or maybe even get the tiniest bit peeved. Even that would be better than this blasé nothingness.

"Well," he finally said, "I think you did the right thing. You handled it very well, and hopefully you've seen the end of it."

She expelled her breath, exasperated. Was that

it? He felt no indignation on her behalf? She opened her mouth to complain, but then she stopped herself. What was she expecting? Paul really didn't know her. Why did she expect him to feel protective of her, just because he was protective of his mother and sister?

But it just grilled her cheese, and she couldn't let it lie. "I think I'm going to have to quit the play."

That got a rise out of him. He nearly slammed on the brakes and finally gave her his full attention.

"What? You mean because of the hand-on-the-knee thing?"

"Yes. The hand-on-*my*-knee thing, to be exact. I can't work for someone who doesn't respect me or my boundaries."

He chuckled, and she didn't like it one bit.

"Look, Anna, I understand how inappropriate Stan's behavior was. It was completely out of line. He's an old coot. He probably comes on to all the young actresses. But he's a good director, from what Mom says. This play is a good opportunity for someone new to the business. Are you sure you want to throw it away?"

She had to breathe deeply to keep from responding with anger. She wasn't going to sell her dignity for the sake of her career. But she didn't want to overreact.

"No, I guess you're right. I don't mean to sound casual about this wonderful chance. I know I would never have even gotten the audition if it hadn't been for your mother."

"She likes you a lot. And she's been talking you up like crazy. You shouldn't let something like a silly gesture by an old man get in the way of your career."

Was this how careers were made here? Did she have to allow dirty old men to fondle her in order to work in the theater? Is that how she wanted to get ahead?

But she kept those concerns to herself. She and Paul clearly looked at this situation in different ways. It made her sad to accept that.

"No, I won't let it get in the way of my career. He probably does do that kind of thing with all of the actresses. One of the more experienced women so much as said so today during our lunch break. It sounded as if Stan might have done something similar in the past. Probably to her. I just didn't understand what she meant until it happened to me."

"There you go. And she's working with him on this new project, right? So he must not take his overtures far. It sounds like you made it clear you were uncomfortable with what he did, so I doubt he'll try anything again. Just shrug him off and enjoy the work."

They neared her building, and she was surprised by her desire to just get away from Paul. And she felt clammy from the nervous perspiration that had persisted since Stan touched her. Her conversation with Paul had done nothing to help that.

"It's early still," Paul said. "You want to get some dinner before going home?" He spoke as if nothing had changed between them. "We could go to that cozy little sushi place down the street."

"I don't think so, Paul." She gathered up her purse and script as if she were going to jump out of the moving car before he could even stop in front of the building. "I guess I'm more tired than I realized. I think I'd just like to stay in and go to sleep early."

"Sure. I understand. Your day started early, didn't it?" He stopped the car and started to get out to open her door.

"No, don't get out, Paul. I'm fine." She opened her own door, and the crisp air blew into the car. "Thanks, though."

But he reached over before she stepped out and placed his warm hand gently on her arm. "Are we okay, Anna? Are *you* okay?"

The worry in his eyes pretty much melted her resolve. She could tell he was genuinely concerned for her. He really was such a kind person. She gave him a smile.

"Everything's fine. Don't worry."

"I'll pick you up in the morning?"

She nodded. "Thanks. Yes, please."

In the elevator Anna almost hit the button to

Edith's floor, thinking maybe she'd feel better if she talked with Edith about what happened with Stan. But she quickly hit the second floor button instead. She was twenty-three, for goodness' sake. Paul was probably right—she needed to shrug off the experience and move on. If she made too big a deal about it, she would signal to everyone that she was a small-town girl too ignorant of the world to make it in New York.

Could You please guide me in this, Lord? I'm not sure how to handle this, and maybe I'm just worrying too much about a minor thing.

Her phone rang right in the middle of her brief prayer. It was her sister, Diane.

"Hey, Anna! You free to talk?"

Anna sighed. "I'm so glad you called, Diane."

"What's up? You don't sound so good."

Diane was only two years younger than Anna. They had always been able to discuss anything with each other, once they survived their teen years and their backbiting moments. Anna told Diane what had happened today, not just with Stan, but with Paul, as well. Diane jumped right on it.

"Anna, you need to come on home. Even if it's just temporary, you need to be with people who love you the right way. That's all messed up, what's going on there. You don't want to work for such a sleazy director. And Paul sounds like a nice enough guy, but he's totally wrong on this."

"I can't just up and leave. I would need to give notice to everyone."

"Well, you have a good excuse to leave quickly. I was actually calling because Dad's in the hospital."

"What? Oh my gosh, I immediately jabbered on about myself, didn't I? Poor Dad! What's wrong?"

"Horrible pain in his stomach area. He couldn't even walk. He was rushed by ambulance about an hour ago. I'm heading there after we hang up—want to grab some of his things for him. Mom's there with him now."

Their father was a cancer survivor, so every scare like this one held more concern than it would have otherwise. Now it felt like more than a coincidence that Diane's call came right on the heels of Anna's prayer.

"Okay," Anna said, "I'm going to see if I can fly out early in the morning. I'll get word to Edith and ask her to relay the info to Paul and to Stan, my lecherous director. Let me go, so I can make some calls. But will you call me if you get more word on Dad?"

"Will do."

By the time Anna dropped off to a restless sleep, she had booked an early morning flight back home and packed enough of her belongings to last her a few days. She didn't like to act irresponsibly with regard to the play, but once she knew about her father's situation, she really didn't care whether or not she lost the part.

Deep down she prayed she wasn't using her father's illness as an excuse to run away from the conflicts that awaited her in the morning.

Chapter Eight

From the moment Anna arrived at the airport, she fidgeted as if she had fleas. There had been no call from Diane yet, and Anna didn't want to wake anyone if they were all at the hospital and had finally dozed off where they sat. She knew Diane would call if there had been news, but still, Anna fussed.

She checked for her phone, for her plane ticket, her boarding pass, her money, her credit card, her script—yes, she had brought her script with her. She hadn't decided, yet, about whether or not she was going to withdraw. If she didn't get fired for leaving town, she needed to be prepared to rehearse if, and when, she returned to New York.

Would Stan be livid? She hated to leave it on Edith to let him know she wouldn't be there, but she didn't yet have a number for Stan. And when she finally worked up the nerve to call Edith this morning, Edith hadn't answered the phone. Anna had left a voice mail, explaining about her sick father. She asked Edith to relay the information to both Stan and Paul.

She fidgeted because she had left what she considered a hint to Edith, in case she decided to withdraw altogether from Stan's play.

"Also, Edith, there's something else I'd like to discuss with you when we have a chance to talk. I'll be sure to call once I know what's happening with my father."

But more than anything, she fidgeted because of Paul. He would hear about Anna's father and her abrupt departure. Edith would likely tell him there was something else Anna wanted to discuss. And he would probably know that something was Stan. If Paul hadn't grasped it yet, he would grasp that despite his assurances and casual reaction to Stan's behavior, Anna was upset enough to possibly leave New York for good.

Or maybe he wouldn't grasp that. Anna liked Paul very much, but she wasn't sure if he was quite in tune with her. She reflected on a moment when they visited Paul's sister, Rachel, and her family in Long Island. She had forgotten about it until this morning.

Anna, Rachel, and Paul had been in the kitchen while Rachel put the meal together. Anna and Paul were helping her in any way they could. At one point, Paul reached out and took a platter from Rachel's hands to carry it out to the table. She didn't let go of it at once, causing him to stop and look her in the eye.

Rachel smiled at him.

He smiled back. "What? What's that grin about?"

She shook her head. "I'm just marveling at how nonchalantly you're pitching in. I didn't even have to ask."

Paul gave her a crooked smile. "Are you being smart?" He headed toward the door, platter in hand.

"Not smart. Really. I'm appreciative." Rachel looked at Anna and winked before speaking loudly enough for Paul to hear in the other room. "Paul's always been a good son to Mom and a good brother to me. But sometimes he just doesn't get it. It never occurred to him that he should help get a meal onto the table—just as much as the womenfolk."

Anna laughed. "Womenfolk."

He walked back into the kitchen, looked at Anna, and gave a little roll of his eyes. "I think it has something to do with my Y chromosome. And Dad's influence."

"Exactly!" Rachel pointed at him and then looked at Anna again. "But Mom finally read him the riot act a little while ago, and he's pitched in ever since. Now he's a good role model for my boys."

Anna saw genuine pleasure in Paul's eyes at that comment.

Rachel continued. "Mom always said Paul might not be perfect, but he was always open to improvement. Educable. Trainable."

Paul gave a little bark that made all three of them laugh.

Now, Anna smiled with the memory. That had been a wonderful day. She had learned more about Paul that weekend than she had any day before or since.

She glanced at her watch. By now Edith would have told him he didn't need to drive Anna to rehearsal. She fought the guilt that wanted to seep into her thoughts. He was a busy man who kept dropping everything to cater to her needs. Hopefully he felt some relief in knowing he could tend straight to his own business today.

But even if that thought wiped away some of her guilty feelings, it also filled her with sadness if he had easily let her go. As if she had been more a burden than a...a what?

The ticket agent called passengers to board. At such short notice Anna had only been able to book a seat on a small, regional airliner, so boarding wouldn't take long.

By the time she settled into her cramped window seat, she managed to stop fidgeting. What was done was done. She had made a choice that might have closed the New-York-theater chapter of her life. For now, anyway. And it most likely closed the chapter of her life involving Paul, too, if such a chapter had ever really been possible.

She was jolted from her relative calm when she looked at the windows of the airport gate from which she and her fellow passengers had just boarded. She saw him run into view and stop. Paul. She saw him approach the window and stare out at her plane.

Whether or not he could see her, she couldn't tell. But she did know he would have had to purchase a plane ticket to get that far past airport security. He had dashed to the airport and bought a ticket so he could catch her before she left town.

She pulled out her phone to see if he had tried to call her. And there it was. How had she missed his call? Would he realize she missed it, or would he think she had ignored it?

She put her hand against the tiny window and tried to make him see her. When he didn't react, she paused for a moment and decided to call him back.

"Please turn off all electronic devices for takeoff." The announcement was followed by a smiling flight attendant who looked directly at Anna and then pointedly at her phone.

She shut down the phone and tucked it into her carry-on bag. The plane slowly taxied away from the gate, and Anna watched Paul at the window until she was forced to turn away and face forward, toward Bethlehem.

Chapter Nine

"Appendicitis." Diane announced it into the phone as soon as she answered Anna's call.

"Why didn't you call me? I've been so worried! His appendix? Is this serious?"

"It's okay, Anna. Take a few breaths. We didn't know until this morning, and he's still in surgery. Or, rather, he's in the recovery room right now. The doctor said it all went well, but it was really bad. Gangrenous. How's that for an early morning picture?"

Anna shuddered. "Poor Dad. I'm at the airport. I'm just waiting for my bag, and then I'll catch a cab to the hospital."

"He'll be so happy to see you. He's not expecting you."

Anna wasn't sure if she would have been so quick to come home had things been going better in New York.

"Hey," she said to Diane, "don't tell him or Mom about what happened with Stan, okay?"

"Got it. I did mention it to Carly, though. I hope you don't mind."

Carly. Just thinking of her made Anna happy. "Gosh, it's been too long. No, I don't mind that you told her. Did you run into her or what?"

"Yeah, she had just come from some parent-teacher thing at the school, and I ran into her at the grocery store. She was buying herself chocolate as a reward for dealing so well with her students' parents. Oh, and she agrees with me. That director guy is creepy. She votes you quit that play. Wait for something better or come on home for good."

"I'm considering my options. Oh, I see my bag. I'll see you in a bit."

"Carly also said not to forget about your cookie exchange thingy."

"Right. But it's only October. That's not 'til Christmas."

"I know. But she said she talked with Kim and Heather recently, and they all wanted you to be sure to come home for your annual whatever."

Anna laughed. "I'm sure I can work that out. Now let me go before someone runs off with my bag. I'll get there as soon as I can."

Despite the circumstances, she smiled at the reminder about the annual cookie exchange she and her childhood friends had celebrated every year for the past decade. No matter what life brought each of them, they touched base each December, exchanging far more than cookies. Divergent paths met on that one night annually, keeping them all grounded and aware of lifelong friendship.

But for now, she had other things to consider. Her father, her career, her dignity. And just for good measure, her...Paul.

~

Anna's appearance at the door to her father's hospital room was the joyous surprise Diane predicted it would be. She received and gave hugs she dearly needed.

"Oh, honey," her father said, "you really didn't have to rush down here for me. This wasn't that serious. The doctor says I'm going to be okay. I'm so sorry."

Anna laughed. "Don't apologize that your condition isn't more serious, Dad. Only you."

"How were you able to get away?" He took a small bite of the colorless meal on the tray in front of him. "I thought you had already started rehearsals."

Anna waved the question away. "Don't worry about that. It's all going to work out just fine." She scrunched her nose. "Why do I smell cabbage if there's no cabbage on that plate?"

Diane eyed the plate, an eyebrow raised. "Troubling."

Anna's phone rang, and she fished it out of her purse. Edith.

"Hey, I'm going to go down to the lobby so I can take this call from Edith. Is that okay with you guys?"

Her father, mother, and Diane all shooed her out of the tiny room.

~

"Darling girl, I got your message." Edith cut right to the matter, as always. "What's the issue you referred to? Tell me the truth."

Anna sighed. Edith was going to think she was such a Podunk hick. "Ugh. I'm sure it will sound silly of me to react this way, Edith. It's just that I experienced some questionable behavior up there, and I—"

"Who was it? Who did what?"

"Well, Stan was—"

"I *knew* it." Edith didn't need much detail, clearly, but Anna didn't want her to think more had happened than that business with her knee.

"It may have been nothing, really, but I'm not comfortable with someone putting his hand on my knee uninvited."

"I could bean him. I could just take a decent-sized phone book and bean the living daylights out of him, I'm telling you."

Anna almost laughed. "It might not have bothered someone more seasoned."

"No, we are not going to make this about your reaction, Anna. I'm calling Stan right now."

"Oh, gosh, I kind of wish you wouldn't, Edith. It's embarrassing for me to not handle this myself."

"Anna, you're not here. You can't handle it yourself."

Anna cringed. Was that criticism?

"And I don't blame you one bit for heading out, especially with your father's issue. Oh, I'm so sorry! I didn't ask. How's he doing, the dear man?"

"He's going to be all right. It was appendicitis, and he's already out of surgery and in recovery."

"God bless him. I prayed for him, you know."

Anna smiled. "I appreciate that, Edith. It helped."

"Well, listen. You spend a few days or so with him and then come on back up, if that's what you want to do. I understand from Gretchen—excellent agent that she is—that they didn't change your lines and they can have someone else read them for the next few days. I don't run the show by any means, but I can tell you right now, that Stan *will* be holding your part open for you for at least a week. That I can see to. And we're going to teach Stan some manners. Don't let this stand in your way, darling. You are a lovely girl. This isn't over."

Anna just loved Edith. "You're way too kind, Edith."

Edith chuckled in her hoarse, smoky voice. "You're my lifesaver, Anna. I'll never forget that."

There was a pause between them, and Anna

suddenly felt as if they were both thinking about the same person at once.

"Edith, I was wondering…

"What were you wondering, dear?"

"Well, when I left New York, when my plane was leaving, I…I actually saw Paul at the gate. Did he happen to say anything to you after I left?"

Another pause ensued, and Anna realized she was gritting her teeth with anxiety.

Finally, a voice so unmistakably full of smile made a quiet pronouncement. "You like my boy."

A flush ran right up Anna's neck, as if Edith were sitting right in front of her. As if *Paul* were sitting right in front of her.

"Um, I believe I do. Yes."

"Well, he was pretty miffed, I have to say, when I saw him today. And I didn't want to press him to tell me what happened between you two. I'm not one to meddle, you know. See, when I got your message, I called and left a voicemail for him that he didn't need to help today, since you were going to be on that early morning flight to Connecticut. I didn't hear a word from him until…well, I guess from what you say, it was after you saw him at the airport. And I guess he came here right from there. I think he's a bit confused."

"Oh. I'm sorry about that."

"Hey, a little confusion is good for him. I love him to death, but things tend to be too easy for him sometimes. Except for that harpy he was with. There was nothing easy about *her*. Not in the good sense of the word, that is."

Anna smiled. No, not meddlesome at all.

"Don't you worry about Paul. Let's take care of your father first. Then Stan. Paul's a big boy. He should take some time to think about what he wants. Anyway, he's got a full plate taking care of my business affairs. I might want him to review my contribution to Stan's production, as a matter of fact."

That made Anna stop the pacing she had begun. "Really?" She felt a clench in her gut. "Edith, if this is too bold, please tell me. But, did I just get this part because of your financial involvement with that play?"

"Not at all, dear. Don't you worry about that. My involvement was only helpful in getting you the audition. Nothing wrong with that. But no director worth his salt is going to cast a no-talent in his play just because one of the contributors wants her auditioned. You earned that part, fair and square. Gretchen told me how wonderful you are. I'm telling you, Anna, this is the place for you. We want you back, as soon as you're ready."

The woman could talk a dead plant into full bloom. Anna wished she could give her a hug.

"Thanks so much, Edith. You're amazing."

"I'm well aware of that, dear. You take care of

your father and come back up here as soon as you can, okay? Promise?"

Suddenly the decision seemed easy. "Promise."

And that was exactly what lingered after Anna ended the call. Promise. In a number of ways.

Chapter Ten

He wasn't Paul.

Anna walked out of the airport without realizing she had assumed Paul would be the one picking her up. This was a perfectly kind-looking, middle-aged gentleman, wearing a dark suit and an actual chauffeur's hat and holding a sign bearing her name. She was ever appreciative that Edith was taking such terrific care of her. But the fact that Paul was suddenly out of the picture wasn't lost on her.

"Ms. Melborn asked that I take you to the apartment so we could drop off your things and let you freshen up if you like. And then I'm to take you to the theater, Stage 47? She's going to meet you there. Is that all right with you, Ms. Chesterfield?"

He took her bag and opened the back door for her. She always rode up front with Paul, so this was just a bit formal and depressing.

"Oh. Yes. Thank you. That's very kind of you. And what's your name, please?"

"Gregory, Miss." He didn't extend his hand to her, but she extended hers to him, so he shook it and gave her a warm smile.

"Please call me Anna, Gregory. And would you mind if I sat up front? I'm not all that comfortable sitting in the back."

"My pleasure, Miss. Uh, forgive me. Anna."

~

Gregory insisted on accompanying Anna up to her apartment so she wouldn't have to carry her luggage. She didn't have much to do before they headed back out to the theater, but she didn't think she'd ever feel ready for the upcoming meeting. So awkward.

"Are you feeling all right, Anna?" Gregory broke the silence after they drove away from the apartment building. "You look anxious. Is there anything I can do for you? You feeling carsick?"

"Oh, gosh, no. That's not the issue. I don't get carsick. I'm just...well, I really hate confrontation. And that's where we're headed right now. To a confrontation."

He nodded. "I see. I don't suppose any person is happy with confrontation. Although I might amend that, if I thought a moment. I've come across a few people who seem to gravitate toward confrontation. Thrive on it."

"Yeah, I guess I have, too."

"But not most of us." His smile and warm

brown eyes nearly calmed her nerves. "Do you want to talk about it? Would that help?"

Anna exhaled. "I'm just not sure about my own sense of judgment right now. I mean, I'm new to Manhattan and the professional theater, and I don't really have a good grasp on the rules and how closely people follow them."

"Rules about…?"

"Appropriate behavior. On the job."

"Ah. Well, judging by the way Ms. Melborn talks about you, I would assume someone *other* than you has been the one to challenge acceptable rules. And I would also assume Ms. Melborn plans to support you in this confrontation. Is that right?"

She shifted in her seat to face him better. What was Gregory doing driving a car? He should be a therapist. "Yes, she does. And I feel like such a child, having her fight my battle."

Neither spoke for a moment. They neared the theater, and Gregory smiled.

"May I make an observation, Anna?"

She lifted her chin toward him. "Fire away."

"You referred to this meeting as your battle. That sounds to me as if you *are* very sure of your sense of judgment. You know where you stand on what's appropriate, and you know where your challenger stands. Whether New York or Connecticut or Timbuktu, I imagine your feelings would be the same."

Anna pondered that. He was right.

"So maybe Ms. Melborn doesn't plan to fight your battle. She may just want to show that you're not alone in it. Maybe she's there just to be a witness for you. There's nothing childish in leaning on good people."

They pulled up in front of the theater. Anna almost felt like hugging Gregory for being so kind. He walked around to her door before she was able to step out, and he extended his hand to her like a complete gentleman.

What a contrast with the way Stan behaved toward her!

"Thanks for that advice, Gregory. I want you to know you helped me. I don't know if I'm still going to have a job when I walk out of this meeting, but I'm determined to say what I need to, either way."

Another thought that Gregory triggered was that Anna was definitely not alone in this "battle," even if Ms. Melborn weren't here to support her. She spent the short walk to the theater communicating with God.

~

And it was in that frame of mind that Anna met Edith in the dark theater lobby.

"Thanks so much for being here for me, Edith."

Edith hooked arms with her. "That's what friends do, dear. Come on. Stan promised to meet us in his little office backstage. And you've probably noticed he's never late."

Anna hadn't really noticed. She had barely interacted with Stan at all so far, so she couldn't have noticed any pattern on his part. Her heartbeat raced as they reached his office door and Edith knocked.

Stan opened the door seconds later and broke into such a friendly smile that Anna wanted to back out at once. Maybe she had misunderstood his gesture. Was she accusing a harmless old man of something that was going to shock and hurt him?

"Edith! Anna! Come in, come in! Anna, how's your father? Better I hope? Come! Sit!"

So solicitous. She felt herself shrinking back from the confident attitude Gregory had instilled in her.

"Thank you, yes. He's in recovery. It was appendicitis."

Stan nodded. "I had that myself a decade or so ago. I'm glad he's all right. We're happy to have you back."

They both looked at Edith, who was uncharacteristically silent. Poker face didn't begin to describe her inscrutable expression.

"So…what's this meeting about?" Stan asked Edith, not Anna.

Now expression blossomed on Edith's face. She squinted her eyes in mock pondering. She tilted her head, jutted out her lips, and then spoke to Stan.

"How about you tell us, Stan? What do you think we might want to discuss? With you." She held out her hands, palms up, and gestured at his small office. "Privately."

The resulting silence was like ants crawling all over one's skin. If Stan didn't speak up, Anna was going to have to burst out with it, herself.

And then she noticed beads of sweat on his upper lip.

He knew exactly why they were there.

He looked at Anna. "Anna, were you uncomfortable with my little gesture the other day? Is that what this is about?"

Edith leaned forward. "I would like to request, Stan, that you reword that question. You think about it. We'll wait." She sat back and crossed her arms.

More silence. Anna wasn't even sure what Edith was driving at, until Stan spoke to her again.

"Did I make you uncomfortable, Anna? I didn't mean to."

Ah. Responsibility. It was as Edith said. This wasn't about Anna's reaction. It was about Stan's behavior. Sharp one, that Edith.

Gregory's supportive words popped into Anna's head.

"Yes. I'm twenty-three, Stan. I'm new to Manhattan. This is my first professional job in the theater. You took advantage of the fact that you're my boss and I want this role. And I don't let anyone touch me like that."

Stan's eyebrows lifted. He sat back in his chair and surveyed Anna. He actually looked proud of her.

"Duly noted. It won't happen again."

"And?" Edith wasn't quite finished with him.

"And...I'm...sorry?"

Edith looked from Stan to Anna, closed her eyes, and shook her head. "Men."

"I am." Stan seemed to sense he had found the right button and simply needed to push it a few more times to make this all go away. "I'm completely sorry."

Anna forced a smile. Why didn't she feel closure with this? "Thanks, Stan. I appreciate that."

Edith stood, so Anna and Stan did as well. Stan looked at Anna.

"So. You'll join us again tomorrow? We're going to start running through the script on stage to get some sense of blocking."

"Uh, sure. I'll be there."

They all turned toward the door. Edith walked out first, and Anna followed her. Anna nearly jumped out of her skin when Stan placed his hand on the small of her back, as if it were necessary to guide her through the door. She walked a little quicker to move away from his touch.

"Thank you, Stan." Edith looked at him briefly before they walked away from him.

"No problem." He remained in the doorway to his office.

Anna almost didn't turn to look at him again, but when she did, he managed to communicate so much with the tiniest gesture.

He winked at her again.

She could have taken a cold glass of water to the face and have been less shocked.

Was the man nervous, stupid, or completely dishonest? And did she want to find out?

TRISH PERRY

Chapter Eleven

Anna was unable to keep from breaking into a broad grin when she and Edith walked out of the theater and she saw the car and driver awaiting them at the curb.

"It's Paul! Uh, I mean—"

Edith chuckled. "It is. He was otherwise engaged earlier, but he harassed me to death for sending Gregory to meet you at the airport, instead of him. He rearranged his schedule so he could be here when we finished with Stan."

Edith stopped at that moment and took hold of Anna by the shoulders. "About that, Anna."

"About Paul?"

A shake of the head. "No. About Stan. I'm not, well, I want to hear what you think. And be perfectly honest with me, if you know how you feel."

"You mean, do I feel comfortable working with him now?"

"Exactly."

Anna took a deep breath as she thought. She felt as if she were ridding herself of pretense as she exhaled.

"Edith, he gives me the creeps."

Edith gave one emphatic nod and patted Anna's arm. "I *knew* you were a smart girl. He gives me the creeps, too."

They both laughed.

"But, if I don't work for him, what will I do?" Anna said. "I can't keep leaning on you for support. I mean, I can toughen up. It's not as if I'm a total innocent. I can stick it out with Stan—"

"Au contraire, my dear. Your innocence is one of my favorite things about you." She tilted her head from side to side. "I know, I know, you *will* toughen up, and you'll learn to diminish little trolls like Stan with a simple arch of a well-groomed eyebrow. But for now? There are other opportunities out there. We've only just begun with you."

"Are you sure?"

"I am. Give me a hug, darling girl. You know you want to."

Anna laughed and wrapped her arms around Edith. "You keep improving my life, Edith. I'm so blessed that I was the one who got your call that night."

"You and me both." Edith pulled back and hooked her arm through Anna's again. "Now let's join Paul. Poor boy, I demanded that he stay with the car and give us privacy when we walked out of the theater. I knew we wouldn't be able to compare notes until then. But I know Paul's like a greyhound at the starting gate right now."

~

Anna and Paul looked at each other as if they were adolescent students at a school dance. But Anna was floored by how great he looked to her. She hadn't realized how sad she had been with the thought of not seeing him again. It didn't hurt that he wore jeans with a V-neck sweater the same gray-blue color as his eyes.

"Hi."

They both said it at the same time. And then they both laughed about that. Paul opened the front passenger door for his mother.

"Here you go, Mom." He smiled from one woman to the other. "You two look like you've got Stan locked up in a steamer trunk back there in the theater."

Edith stopped short of getting into the car. "You know what, honey? I think I'll go back in there and have a little more of a chat with Stan. He's going to have to make some arrangements he doesn't know about yet, so I think I'll give him a heads-up."

"Okay," Paul said. "We'll wait for you here, unless you want me to walk you in."

Edith waved him off. "No, no, you kids go.

Talk. " She smiled at Anna before looking back at Paul. "Apologize. That kind of thing. I'll text Gregory to come get me."

Paul gave Anna a crooked smile before addressing his mother again.

"Well, at least let me walk you in, Mom."

"I'm fifty-nine, darling, not ninety-nine. You watch me now. I can amble back in there with the best of them."

"But, Edith," Anna said, "don't you think I should be the one to talk with Stan?"

"Oh, sure, you can follow up. I have a few other words for him besides the ones you need to say. I'm one of his investors, after all. I care about the artists my money supports."

~

Paul hadn't driven halfway towards Anna and Edith's apartment building before changing course.

"Would you mind if we took a little walk? And talk?"

She realized he had turned toward Central Park. They had taken a number of walks in the park during her months in Manhattan. It was always a treat. The leaves were especially pretty now, their fall color ablaze.

"No, I'd like that."

There was a chill in the air, and Anna pulled her jacket closed as they walked through the park. She had a sense Paul might put his arm around her to warm her up. But considering the conflict they had been through recently, it might have seemed inappropriate.

"I was wrong to take your feelings so lightly last week," he said. Even though they were walking, he looked directly at her for a moment. She appreciated that about him. Eye contact seemed important to him. "I'm not sure if it's because I'm a guy or because I've grown up here, where attitudes can be cynical. Or because I'm just an idiot."

She smiled. She was looking at the pavement, but she returned the courtesy and looked over at him.

"But it's your fault too, Anna."

She stopped walking. "My fault? What did *I* do?"

"It's what you *didn't* do. You weren't totally honest with me. I asked you if we were okay and if *you* were okay. I really wanted to know. And you just told me you were fine and not to worry. Your way of telling me the truth—by running off to Connecticut—was a little passive-aggressive, don't you think? I was an idiot, but at least I was an honest idiot."

Of all the nerve. Eye contact was simple after that. She wanted to shoot daggers from hers.

"Well, it was perfectly obvious how you felt about the whole thing, Paul. You even laughed at me for being upset about that lascivious geezer groping me. There didn't seem to be any point trying to convince you otherwise. Anyway, I think I was pretty clear about how upset I was."

"At first, yes, but then after we talked, you said you were fine. If I had known you weren't, I would have—"

"You would have dismissed my feelings even more. You would have tried even harder to persuade me about how wrong or silly I was. Anything other than respecting me enough to accept that how I felt was *real*."

She noticed her voice had become loud, her lips thin and tight.

In the silence, they both glanced around themselves. If anyone nearby was interested in their squabble, they hid it well.

Paul breathed audibly, a long sigh. He shook his head and looked at the ground between them.

Here they went. He was going to give up. And maybe that was for the best. She was actually relieved she had been able to express why she was angry with him, even if it was going to destroy them.

"You are so right."

She frowned, puzzled. "What do you mean?"

He looked up at her, self-deprecating resignation all over his face. "That's exactly what I would have done. I'm so sorry. I didn't want you to be upset, so I figured I could talk you out of it. That wasn't what you needed."

She had to stop herself from dismissing her feelings again, from telling him that, no, no, it was all right, she didn't mind the way he had reacted to her concerns. What was *wrong* with her? Instead, she just affirmed what he said. "No. That wasn't what I needed."

"What you needed was for me to grasp how you felt."

"Um, yes."

Still, this wasn't *all* about how poorly he had handled their last conversation.

"But...now that you're being so nice, Paul, I'll admit that I should have been more frank about wanting to get away from you, there at the end."

She thought she heard a gasp from him before he caught himself.

"Really? It was that bad?"

She shrugged. She figured she might as well bet the whole farm at this point. "I was pretty mad. I thought you were being insensitive. I don't want an insensitive boyfriend."

Paul grimaced. "Okay, I get that, I deserve that. But would you do me a favor and go ahead and fling it in my face next time? Like, when it's actually happening, as opposed to a week or so later?"

"Okay. Wait. Next time?" Anna had fun arching that brow, as Edith had described.

Now Paul showed total confidence. "Oh, I can guarantee there will be a next time. I'm not exactly a savant in the sensitivity department. So my sister tells me."

Anna couldn't keep a smile from pulling at her lips. She started to walk so she didn't have to look directly at him. "I like Rachel. She's a smart woman."

She heard him chuckle as he joined her.

Now it didn't seem at all odd when Paul tentatively put his arm around her. They walked further before either of them spoke again.

"I was shocked when you suddenly left town," Paul said. "I mean, I was pretty…upset."

"I know."

"Mom told you?"

"Yeah. But I could tell before that."

"What do you mean? We hadn't talked."

"I saw you. At the airport window. At my gate."

"You could see my expression all the way over there? From the plane?"

"Body language, Paul. You looked like a puppy in a pet shop window."

"Hey!"

"Cold, moist nose up against the window, drooping ears and shoulders, whimpering…"

He laughed. "There wasn't a single whimper, believe me. Not until I got back to my car."

Anna laughed. "I promise to be more frank with

you from now on."

"Good. I think. And I'll try not to be a bonehead."

"Please. And I do appreciate that my task will be easier than yours."

They both laughed, and he squeezed her closer to him. "Boyfriend, huh?"

"You caught that, did you?"

"I did." He stopped her again, but he didn't remove his arm. Rather, he faced her and wrapped both arms around her. He touched his forehead to hers.

"Honestly, Anna, I know we've only known each other, what, five months or so? But at that airport gate, when I thought maybe I wouldn't see you again, I was a wreck. It hit me so abruptly. Like I had fallen off a cliff and couldn't get my footing. I felt like the most important person in my life had left on that plane."

Heat flushed all over Anna's cheeks as she looked into his eyes, so close to hers. "Whoa."

He pulled away. "Too much?"

She shook her head. "Juuuuust right."

Paul kissed her gently. In the chilly air, the soft warmth of his lips was more than perfect.

Her eyes still closed, Anna smiled. "Even better."

Chapter Twelve

Two months later, Anna arrived back in Bethlehem, but this time her return home was a pleasure. She had one week free for the Christmas holiday. A light snow fell in New York as her plane lifted off, and the same had happened as she landed in Connecticut. Even though the sun was out, the air was cold enough that the soft, quiet snow remained, sparkling like glitter.

Her mother turned to face her in the car as they neared town. "When are you getting together with Carly and the other girls for your cookie exchange?"

"Oh! Thanks for the reminder. Could we swing by the grocery store before we go home? I need to get the ingredients for my Chocolate Peppermint Bars. We're meeting at my apartment—I mean, Diane's apartment—tomorrow night, so I'd like to get those made today."

Her father met her eye in the rearview mirror. "Is Diane joining you girls for your slumber party this year, then? It's nice of you to include your sister in the group."

Anna smiled. "Diane doesn't need my friends. She's perfectly happy with the masses of friends she already has. I don't think she'll be back from her business trip by tomorrow, will she? That was kind of the point of her offering her place to us."

"That's right," Anna's mother said. "Remember, Doug? She doesn't get back until the twenty-second." She turned back to Anna. "Are you sure you're all right with Diane taking over the lease on your apartment, honey?"

"Absolutely." Anna scanned her phone for the list of ingredients she needed from the grocery store. "Everything is looking really good for New York. Edith is going to rent that awesome apartment to me for as long as I need it, and I know she's giving me a ridiculously low rate." She looked up at her mother. "Mom, she's like an angel in my life, you know?"

Her mother's eyes twinkled. "Ours, too. When you have kids of your own you'll know how much peace you feel when your kids are happy. Someday I want to meet Edith."

They pulled into the grocery store parking lot. "That will definitely happen. I'll be right back."

~

The following night, Anna walked into her old apartment and grinned at the touches Diane had made. Diane was a freak about the color blue, and there were accents of it everywhere. Somehow it gave a more contemporary feel to the place. Anna appreciated how tidy the apartment looked too. When they were teens and shared a room, Diane's side was always insanely cluttered. Either she had turned a new leaf, or she had taken the time to de-clutter before she left on her business trip. Either way, the circumstances showed Diane had matured since moving out of the family home.

Anna got the heater going, set out the scented candles she had brought, warmed the spiced cider, and started a pot of coffee.

Carly was the first to arrive, and she and Anna nearly cried when they hugged.

"Oh, Anna, I've missed having you right around the corner!" Carly dropped her sleeping bag in the living room, pulled off her coat and hat, and took her overnight case into the bedroom. She and Anna used to hang out in the apartment constantly before Anna moved to New York, so Carly was completely at home. "It's so odd to think that this isn't going to be your place anymore. It doesn't feel right."

"But it *is* right, Carly! I really love New York. I feel so blessed that things have turned out the way they have."

They both turned to look at the front door when a quick knock preceded Kim and Heather's entrance. All four of the women emitted delighted squeals and had a little hug fest while juggling containers of cookies, sleeping bags, and gifts.

In no time, they had changed into their pajamas, laid out sleeping bags and cookies and other goodies for the evening, and started filling each other in on the events of the previous year. Each woman had her share of joys and sorrows to share. Anna was thrilled to have good news to report. That might not have been the case had they gathered during her trip home just months ago.

Kim set down her cider and hugged her knees. "So, Anna, you managed to find another play after quitting the one directed by the dirty old man?"

Anna laughed. "It took a month or so, but yes. This one is a little farther off Broadway, but I'm so happy with the role. I have a few more lines than I did in the other play, and the director is *so* creative. And he's completely respectable. His wife is in the play, as well. Very cool couple."

"So when is opening night?" Heather pulled out her phone and acted very official. "I'm going to make sure it doesn't conflict with my exam schedule, and I'll need to make sure the fam can keep Jenna for me. We girls should come up to see you, lady."

"Road trip!" Carly announced. "I can't wait! I need this—" she worked her hand around the circle to include all four of them—"for a bit longer than one night, after spending so much time with the wee ones at school! Adult conversation! Yes!"

Anna grinned. "The opening is in late January. I'll text you the dates tomorrow. That would be so terrific, if you could all come up. And I'd like you to meet Edith and Paul."

Kim sighed. "I doubt I'll be able to make it to New York from Detroit next month. Just getting time off to come home for the holidays was an undertaking." She smiled. "But I'll be there in spirit."

Heather said, "So, Edith is your benefactor, and Paul is—"

"Her *benefactor*." Carly wiggled her eyebrows at them all.

Everyone laughed. Anna said, "I don't even know what that's supposed to mean, woman." She pointed at Carly's eyebrows, frowning. "But I have to admit, I've definitely benefitted from meeting *both* Edith and Paul. I don't know if I've ever met a more generous person than Edith."

Kim gave her an eager smile. "And Paul? I want to hear about him."

Anna sighed, a smile spreading her lips. "We're still getting to know each other. But he's...he's really a good guy. He could be so different. His parents became pretty rich when he was still young. He could have turned out spoiled or snooty. But Edith and her husband definitely had the parenting thing down pat. He has *so* much love and respect for his mother. He's a savvy businessman too, totally responsible. And as his sister said, he's so open to…being…taught."

"Taught?" Carly tilted her head. "By you, you mean?

Anna shrugged. "Me, Edith, father figures, whatever. He wants to be the best man he can be. He has no pride about that. Not that I can see, anyway."

"I love him already." Kim grinned. "Any brothers?"

"Only a sister. Sorry."

Heather nodded. "Okay, so let's get down to it. How about the kissing? Is he a good kisser?"

Anna decided to have fun with them. She dramatically lowered her head, shook it one time, smacked her hand on the coffee table, and said, "Mercy!"

They erupted in laughter, not unlike the giggles they had shared during Christmases past, when they were still adolescent girls.

"Honestly, though," Anna said. "We're taking it slowly on that front. He was in a pretty awful relationship that was just ending when I moved up there. And we're both busy and focused on doing well in our jobs. He runs all of Edith's financial affairs, which is apparently a tall order. But…I'm actually not kidding on the whole *mercy* thing. He is *gorgeous*. Light blue eyes, dark hair, toned like an athlete."

In the midst of the laughing and conversations that followed, Anna sensed a warmth all over. She hadn't actually been in a position to talk about Paul with anyone since the two of them had become an "item." Not this way, at least. Edith knew, of course, that they were growing closer and closer to each other, and she clearly approved. And the friends Anna was developing in New York knew Paul and her as a couple, but they had never known them any other way.

These three women, though, had known her as a friend for more than a decade. They knew what her dreams had been, both professionally and personally. So they knew how special her emerging career was, and they appreciated how important was her blossoming relationship with Paul.

Until tonight she hadn't realized how much she wanted to talk about him with someone who truly knew her. For a reason she couldn't quite grasp, talking about him this way made her feel even closer to him. It was all she could do to refrain from leaving the room, calling him up, and proclaiming, "This thing we have, you and me? I think this thing is real."

Chapter Thirteen

The enthusiastic applause continued to

play in Anna's mind as she walked out to the theater lobby. Opening night had been a success, and everyone still at the theater buzzed with excitement. Anna kept grinning over the fact that one of her lines got such a huge laugh, as it was meant to do. How amazing that she would probably get that reaction every time they performed the play. This was one of many reasons she had gone into theater. The feedback was addicting and an immediate reward for a job well done.

"Oh, honey!" Her mom and dad awaited her in the lobby. And then she saw everyone else at once. She found herself in a virtual hugging conga line, bouncing from her mom to her dad, to Diane, and then to Heather and Carly, who had managed to make it to New York to support her. As Kim had predicted, she had been unable to leave Detroit but had sent a sweet note to lend her support.

Anna was truly blessed.

Edith approached her, her arm linked with Isaac Thornberg's, the play's producer. The two of them looked like cats who had caught the canary, and Anna knew exactly how they felt.

Edith gave her a wink but spoke to Isaac. "Did I not tell you and Leo that this lovely girl was one to watch?"

Isaac smiled at Anna. "You did. And Leo told me you're a pleasure to direct, Anna. I think you're going to do well. I hope so."

"Thanks, Mr. Thornberg. I hope so, too. I love the play."

As Edith and Isaac started to move toward another person in the crowd, Edith spoke over her shoulder to Anna.

"I have to do a little schmoozing here. I'll see you back at my apartment? You bringing your family and your girlfriends?"

"We'll be there!"

Edith had planned a small gathering at her place to celebrate the play's opening night. She had told Anna and Paul not to worry if they got there before she did. She had a catering company already there.

"And the Tony goes to..." The official-sounding, deep voice behind Anna made her smile before she turned around.

She and Paul put their arms around each other.

"You were even better than I expected." Paul's crystal blue eyes twinkled with pride. "You're funny! Who knew?"

She drew closer to hug him. "Thank you so much for always being there to cart me around town and tell me what I needed to hear."

His soft laugh rumbled against her. "Maybe not *always* what you needed to hear, huh?"

She pulled back and was about to answer when her mother, father, and sister walked up. Her father put out his hand.

"So you're the young man who's caught my daughter's eye, I take it? Doug Chesterfield."

"Paul Melborn, sir. And I certainly hope I'm that young man." They shook hands, and then Paul enveloped Anna's mother's hand in both of his. "Welcome to New York, Mrs. Chesterfield."

"Oh, call me Shelly. And this is Anna's sister, Diane."

Diane's frank and ever-upbeat attitude was front and center. "Well, I can certainly see why Anna was so eager to get back up here after Christmas. You are *really* easy on the eyes, aren't you?" Anna saw her grimace at what was, apparently, a subtle pinch from her mother.

Shelly interrupted. "It's been ages since we've been up here," she said. "I just love Manhattan. And we're eager to get to know you a little better. And your wonderful mother."

Paul glanced over the crowd. "I think she wants us to go ahead to her place. She has a little thing put together for us there. She'll be right behind us."

Edith had provided a limo for them to ride over, so the available cookie exchange members joined them for a very high-class trip across town. By the time they arrived at Edith and Anna's building, everyone had been introduced to Paul, who clearly charmed them all.

The apartment was elegantly lit, and soft music played over the sound system as they entered. Although Edith's Christmas décor had been removed weeks before, delicate white lights draped beautifully around the room, casting it in a magical glow. Along the dining table were platters of simple but delicious hors d'oeuvres and pastries.

Edith arrived shortly after the rest of them. She immediately became the charming hostess and made sure everyone was entertained and happy.

Her arrival gave Paul and Anna the opportunity to grab their coats and step out on the balcony for a few moments alone. As was always the case, a lot of light and life continued on the street below them. New York truly was the never-sleeping city. But Anna and Paul experienced a kind of intimacy, shut away from family and friends by the simple sliding door to Edith's apartment.

They stood side-by-side and leaned against the balcony rail. They looked out on the city for a few silent moments before Paul put his arm around her.

"Rachel and Michael send their apologies for

not being able to drive in for your opening."

Anna had only visited with Paul's sister and her husband twice since their initial meeting in Long Island, but she found them and their kids very easy to love.

"That's really sweet of them to even consider it."

He nodded. "They lost their regular babysitter and have to find a new victim before they can do anything apart from their crazy brood. Next week or so, maybe."

"That'll give us time to get some of the kinks out of the play."

He turned his head to make eye contact with her. "I was teasing before, you know, about being surprised by your being funny."

"I know."

"Your sense of humor is one of my favorite things about you. Too many people lose that when they live in the city. Any busy city, really."

She looked back over the streets. "Hmm. I guess so. People get cynical." She glanced back at him. "But you don't seem all that cynical."

He chuckled. "I think I'm less cynical since meeting you. You woke me up to a few things about kindness and respect for people."

"Watch out, now. I have to be able to fit my head back through that sliding glass door."

Paul turned to face her and pulled an oblong box

from his coat pocket. "I got you a little something to celebrate your opening night."

A ring box would have sent her into a panic—far, far too soon. But the oblong box brought true joy to her.

"Oh my gosh, Paul. Talk about kindness."

She opened the box to see a delicate gold heart pendant necklace. She gasped with pleasure.

"You like it?"

"I love it! Thank you. It's so feminine!"

He turned her around to face away from him. She lifted her hair, and he clasped the chain behind her neck. "Well, I almost got the big rhinestone-covered 'New York' letters like the rappers wear. But the price on this was better."

She turned back around and shook her head at him. "Is that so?"

"Anyway, you seem to have this thing about hearts."

She tilted her head and gave him a puzzled look. "What are you talking about?"

He shrugged. "I know my mother's life—like yours, like mine—is completely in God's hands. But, you know, in a way, on that day this summer, when you answered Mom's phone call? You gave her heart back to her."

She opened her mouth to protest, but he gave her a subtle shake of the head.

"Don't argue with me on this. You did. We've

discussed this before. Others wouldn't have done what you did. You gave her heart back to her."

He lifted her hands to his lips and kissed them once, gently. "And then you turned right around and stole mine."

The playfulness had gone from his eyes, and she wasn't sure if she'd ever had anyone look at her with such gravity. Such soul.

She felt the sting of tears, shocked at how quickly he had managed to touch her. "How about I keep it, then?"

"My heart?" He nodded. "Yes."

"And how about you keep mine?"

He said nothing. He released her hands and reached up to cup her face. He leaned in to kiss her as a gentle snow began to fall, the flakes melting on their skin.

Anna's Chocolate Peppermint Bars

FIRST LAYER
2   squares unsweetened chocolate
1   stick butter
2   eggs, beaten
1   cup sugar
½   cup sifted flour
½   cup chopped, unblanched almonds

Melt chocolate and butter over hot water; blend together. Separately, combine eggs and sugar. Beat until sugar is dissolved. Add flour to eggs, then nuts and chocolate mixture. Mix thoroughly.

Preheat oven to 350 degrees. Line an 8-inch square pan with greased foil. Overlap edges of foil so it may be lifted from pan to facilitate cutting of bars. Add batter, spreading it evenly over bottom of pan.

Bake on lower shelf of oven for 20 minutes. Transfer to center of oven and continue to bake about five minutes or until done. Cool.

SECOND LAYER

1 ½   cups powdered sugar
3   tablespoons softened butter
1 ½   tablespoons half and half
1   teaspoon peppermint flavoring
     few drops green food coloring

Combine sugar and butter, mixing until smooth.
Blend in cream, peppermint, and food coloring, mixing
again until smooth. Spread on cooled first layer as
smoothly and evenly as possible. Refrigerate until
chilled.

THIRD LAYER

1 ½   squares unsweetened chocolate
1 ½ tablespoons melted butter

Melt chocolate and butter over hot water; blend
together. Spread over second layer as smoothly as
possible with spatula. Chill. Cut into bars about 1 x 2
inches each. Yields about 32 bars.

Freeze well. Keep wrapped in foil.

About Trish Perry

Award-winning novelist Trish Perry has written A Special Kind of Double (2019), A Midnight Clear, Together by Design (2018), Local Girl, Miss Apprehension (2017), Under the Dogwood Tree (2016), and Love's First Stage (2015) for Forget-Me-Not Romances; More Than Meets the Eye for Mountain Brook Ink (2016); Unforgettable (2011, Summerside Press); and Tea for Two (2011), The Perfect Blend (2010), Sunset Beach (2009--winner, 2010 Greater Detroit RWA Award), Beach Dreams (2008), Too Good to Be True (2007), and The Guy I'm Not Dating (2006), all for Harvest House Publishers. She collaborated with several renowned authors on the devotionals Grace is Like Chocolate without the Calories for Worthy (2017), Better Than Chocolate for Broadstreet (2015), the Be Still...and Let Your Nail Polish Dry Journal for Ellie Claire (2015), as well as Delight Yourself in the Lord...Even on Bad Hair Days (Spring 2011) and His Grace is Sufficient...Decaf is NOT (Fall 2011) for Summerside Press. Her short Christmas novel, 'Tis the Season, is featured in Summerside's Love Finds You on Christmas Morning (2011), along with Debby Mayne's Deck the Halls. And her novella, Labor of Love, is included in The Midwife's Legacy, released June 2012 by Barbour.

Perry wrote a monthly column, "Real Life is Stranger," for Christian Fiction Online Magazine and was editor of Ink and the Spirit, the newsletter of Washington D.C.'s Capital Christian Writers organization, for seven years. Before her novels, Perry published numerous short stories, essays, devotionals, and poetry in Christian and general market media.

Perry holds a B.A. in Psychology, was a 1980s stockbroker, and held positions at the Securities and Exchange Commission and in several Washington law firms. She served on the Board of Directors of CCW and is a member of American Christian Fiction Writers. She invites you to visit her at www.trishperry.com

Printed in Great Britain
by Amazon

76219260R00066